Bear Grylls

GOING CAMPING

Bear Grylls

This survival handbook has been specially put together to help young adventurers just like you to stay safe in the wild. Camping in the great outdoors can be one of the most rewarding experiences—as long as you are fully prepared for a night under the stars. Once you know how to build a campfire, safely store food, and build your shelter you can embark on great adventures!

Bear.

CONTENTS

GOING CAMPING!

Camping with friends and family can be a mini-adventure! A good campsite will allow you to enjoy your surroundings and will be kind to the environment. You should also be able to relax there safely. Take the time to fully prepare for your trip and you'll make great memories in the outdoors.

Making camp

Camp at existing campsites when possible, and remember that good campsites are found, not made.

take note of the wind direction

pitch your tent on clear, level ground a safe distance from any fires

place a toilet 500 feet from water

BEAR SAYS

Camping is a great way to enjoy the outdoors and experience nature at its best!

Places to avoid

Some locations are not good for camping—stay away at all costs!

Flood risk

Washouts, gullies, and floodplains can be deadly when it rains.

Under a tree

Even healthy-looking branches may drop without warning.

Cliff base

Don't camp below a cliff or a steep, rocky slope in case loose rocks fall.

Avalanche risk

Stay away from steep slopes during or after heavy snowfall.

TENTS

A tent is your home away from home while camping. It shelters you from wind, rain, cold temperatures, and blazing sun. There are lots of different types to choose from.

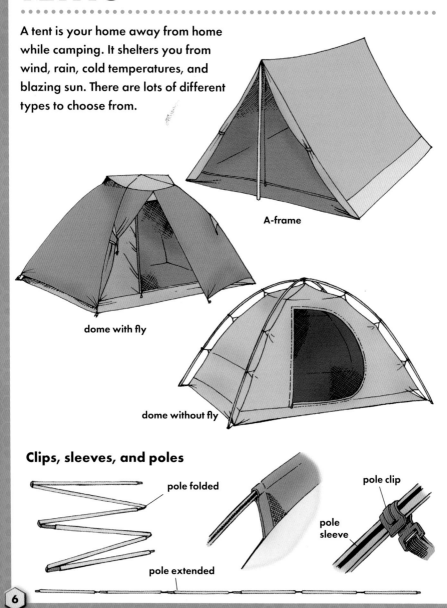

A-frame

dome with fly

dome without fly

Clips, sleeves, and poles

pole folded

pole extended

pole sleeve

pole clip

pole sleeve

geodesic

two-hoop

three-hoop

family

self-erecting

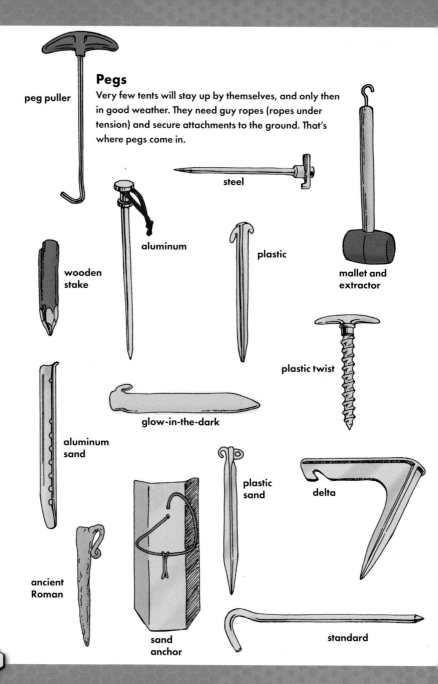

Pegs

Very few tents will stay up by themselves, and only then in good weather. They need guy ropes (ropes under tension) and secure attachments to the ground. That's where pegs come in.

peg puller

steel

aluminum

plastic

mallet and extractor

wooden stake

plastic twist

aluminum sand

glow-in-the-dark

ancient Roman

sand anchor

plastic sand

delta

standard

Placing pegs

It is important to make sure your tent is stable and stays put so that you have proper shelter.

Mountain favorite

A buried sleeping bag case filled with snow makes a good anchor.

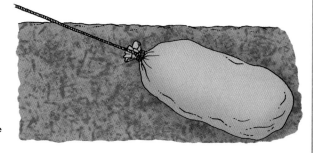

Standard

The rope is at 90 degrees to the peg.

Super stable

When stability is key, use two pegs for extra security.

Delta

These strong pegs keep a very secure hold.

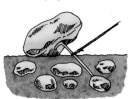

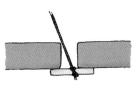

Backup

Use a heavy rock to secure a peg if it won't go far into the ground.

Rocks

Piles of rocks can be used to anchor your lines.

Ice

A tent peg can be placed in a hole in the ice.

Desert sand

A peg buried in sand makes a good anchor.

Buried in ice

A peg can be frozen in ice to secure its hold.

Parachute

Place heavy objects in a parachute anchor, then bury.

What to do if your tent leaks

If you expect wet weather or a downpour looms, these simple tips can save the day.

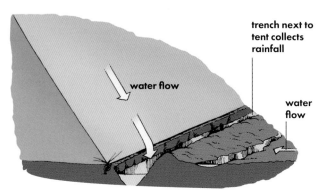

trench next to tent collects rainfall

water flow

Water trench

A bit of digging can help avoid a flood in your tent.

water flow

Inside drip string

This short-term fix allows leaking water to drip into a bowl rather than your sleeping bag.

string

Outside string

This diverts water from reaching the anchor point of your tent or tarp.

stone

Duct tape

Apply to a hole or split seam.

Hole patch

Patch kits will securely seal a leaking hole.

Seam sealer

Use a sealer for leaks along the seam.

OTHER TYPES OF SHELTERS

From tarpaulin to igloos, there are many other types of shelters that could be a better option than a tent.

The art of tarp
These are some ways tarpaulin can be made into a shelter.

pyramid

a tied-off rock will work as a corner anchor

A-frame

lean-to

BEAR SAYS
A tensioner will maintain tension in a guy rope. They are simple yet important pieces of gear—I never go camping without them!

Plastic line
A small tug on this tensioner will tighten the guy ropes.

Timber line
A piece of timber with two holes will also hold guy ropes in place.

grommet

Stick anchor
This simple method will save wear on your tarp's corner grommets.

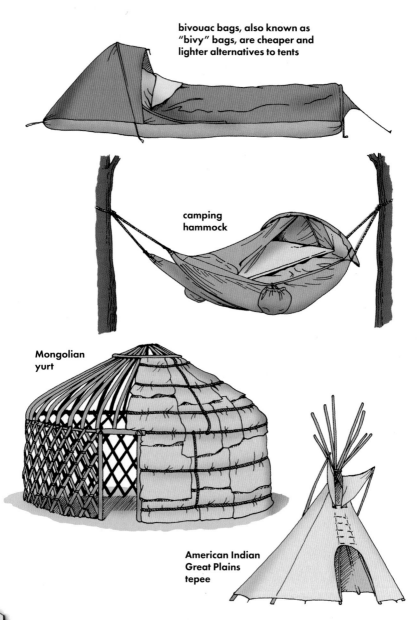

bivouac bags, also known as "bivy" bags, are cheaper and lighter alternatives to tents

camping hammock

Mongolian yurt

American Indian Great Plains tepee

Snow cave

With experience and a snow shovel, you and a friend can build a comfortable snow cave in a couple of hours. This can be a lifesaver, but you have to be careful of carbon monoxide gas poisoning.

ventilation hole

skis or other equipment can alert your position to others

Igloo

This Inuit invention is an option for shelter in cold conditions.

BEAR SAYS

Snow is a great insulator in freezing conditions. Once you have made your shelter, compress snow into blocks to seal up the entrance.

How to make an igloo

1 Mark a circle in the snow about 7 feet across.

2 Tramp down the snow inside the circle until you have a solid surface.

1. To make a snow block, first cut two parallel lines

snow saw

3. Lastly, make a vertical cut

2. Then make a horizontal cut

3 Using a snow saw, cut blocks of hard, compacted snow. Hard snow can usually be found below soft snow.

5 Cut a ramp in the snow blocks halfway around the circle.

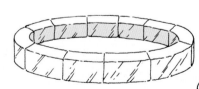

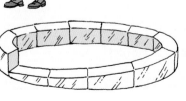

4 Arrange your first blocks in a circle.

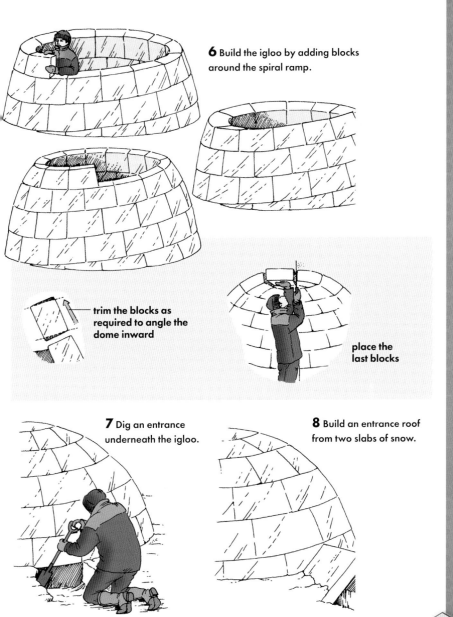

6 Build the igloo by adding blocks around the spiral ramp.

trim the blocks as required to angle the dome inward

place the last blocks

7 Dig an entrance underneath the igloo.

8 Build an entrance roof from two slabs of snow.

How to make a quinzee

A quinzee is a large pile of snow that has been hollowed out.

1 Put backpacks and any other bulky gear together.

2 Pile up a good-sized amount of snow over your backpacks.

3 Pack down the snow and wait a couple of hours while it "sinters" (this is when the snow crystals bind to each other).

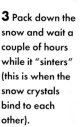

4 Stick even-lengthed sticks all around the snow pile.

5 Excavate the snow. The other ends of the sticks will guide you and keep you from digging through.

air hole

6 Insulate the base with tarps or sleeping mats, and make yourself at home.

SLEEPING SOFTLY

A camping mattress makes sleeping more comfy, and also keeps you warmer than if you were to sleep directly on the ground.

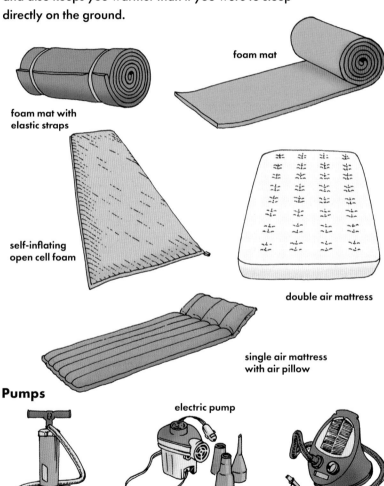

foam mat

foam mat with elastic straps

self-inflating open cell foam

double air mattress

single air mattress with air pillow

Pumps

electric pump

hand pump

foot pump (uses bellows)

SLEEPING BAGS

A good-quality sleeping bag is essential for a good night's sleep in the outdoors.

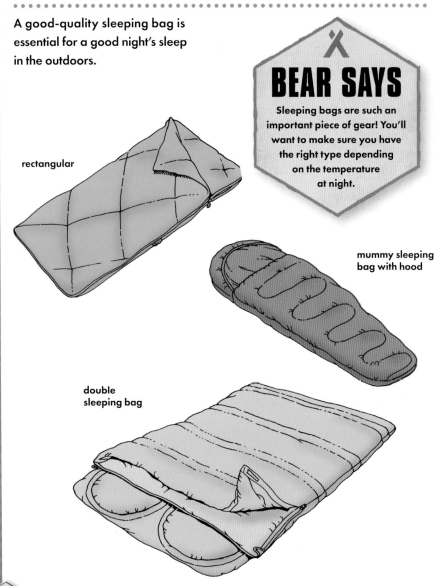

BEAR SAYS

Sleeping bags are such an important piece of gear! You'll want to make sure you have the right type depending on the temperature at night.

rectangular

mummy sleeping bag with hood

double sleeping bag

18

compression sack

stuff bag

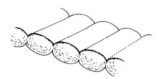

Sleeping bag fillings

A sleeping bag is made up of a lining and an outer shell. In between the two are different types of filling. The way in which the filling is stitched together affects how warm you stay inside it. Down bags are also often built with pockets called baffles that stop the down from bunching.

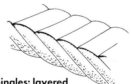

sewn through: outer shell is stitched together

offset quilt: staggered double layers

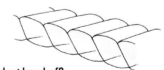

shingles: layered like roof tiles

box-shaped baffle

slant box baffle

trapezoidal baffle

V-tube baffle

KNIVES

A good sharp knife is a camping essential, but should only be used by an adult with caution and care.

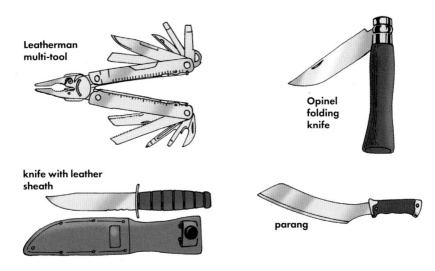

Leatherman multi-tool

Opinel folding knife

knife with leather sheath

parang

Survival knife

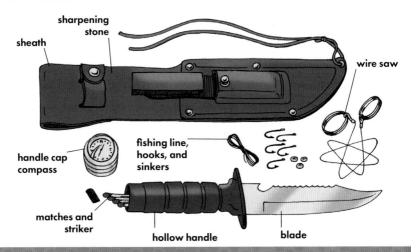

sheath

sharpening stone

wire saw

handle cap compass

fishing line, hooks, and sinkers

matches and striker

hollow handle

blade

Swiss Army knife

Boy Scout knife

folding knife

✖ BEAR SAYS

Knives can have fixed or
folding blades, and
often come with other
tools too.

Parts of a hunting knife

hilt

rivets

blade

thumb grip

spacer

handle

tang

rivet hole

assembled knife

Knife sharpening

To sharpen a knife, the blade is often passed over a hard, rough surface.

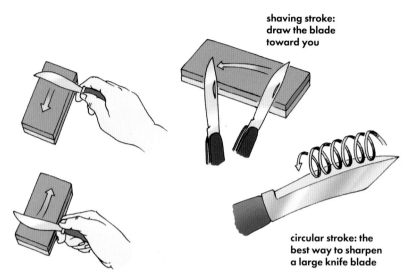

shaving stroke: draw the blade toward you

circular stroke: the best way to sharpen a large knife blade

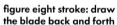

figure eight stroke: draw the blade back and forth

Useful tools

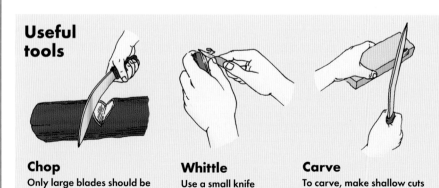

Chop
Only large blades should be used for chopping.

Whittle
Use a small knife for fine carving.

Carve
To carve, make shallow cuts along the grain.

honing oil

honing stone

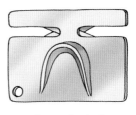

sharpening tool

sharpening steel

BEAR SAYS

Knives are very useful pieces of equipment and require a lot of special care.

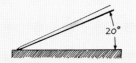

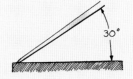

10 degrees
For light duty and fine work such as filleting and shaving. The edge will blunt fairly quickly.

20 degrees
A good angle for everyday use. To approximate it, imagine half of 90 degrees, then half of 45 degrees.

30 degrees
A somewhat blunt yet long-lasting edge for heavy-duty work, such as chopping wood.

TOILETS AND SHOWERS

For a healthy environment and a healthy you, make sure you maintain good hygiene by washing and showering. Depending on your needs, there are different types of toilets that can be built outdoors.

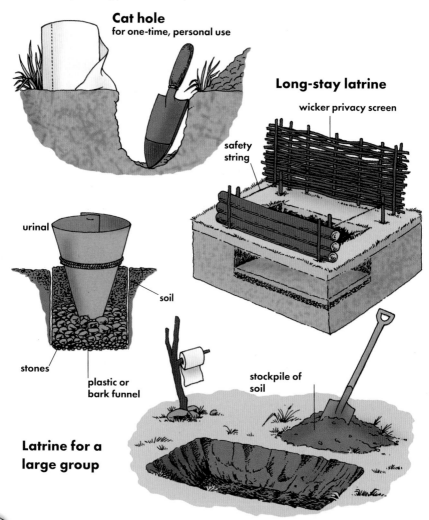

Cat hole
for one-time, personal use

Long-stay latrine

wicker privacy screen

safety string

urinal

soil

stones

plastic or bark funnel

stockpile of soil

Latrine for a large group

Keeping clean

bar soap

hand soap

antibacterial wipes

Using a solar shower

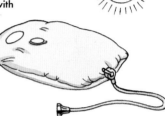

1 Fill the shower bag with water and lay it in the sun. On a cool or overcast day, do this in the morning so that there is warm water in the afternoon.

2 Hang the bag from a tree. The bag will be heavy, so pick a branch that is strong and healthy.

3 Check that the water is at a safe temperature before starting your shower.

you could hang a curtain for privacy

BEAR SAYS

Staying clean may not always be an obvious part of survival, but without it hygiene will suffer, making infections more likely.

FOOD CACHES

You don't want to share your precious food supplies with the local wildlife. In some places hungry bears may look for a meal.

BEAR CACHES

Traditional cache

These mini log cabins are raised up high off the ground. They are still used in North American woods.

removable ladder

Camping ground cache

These permanent bear-proof cabinets are a common sight in camping grounds where bears might visit.

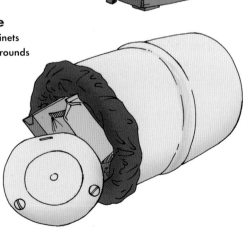

Bear can

These tough canisters can hold about a week's worth of food for the average hiker.

Setting up a throw line bear cache

secure your food bag to the line

1 Find two trees about 15 feet apart. Throw the rope up and over a branch.

2 Tie the rope to the tree trunk, then throw the rope over a branch on the second tree.

3 Then, hoist it up until it's at least 12 feet above the ground.

4 Tie the other end of the line to the trunk of the second tree. Your food is now safe.

BEAR SAYS

Bears have an incredible sense of smell, and are also able to recognize the sight of food containers.

stones

throw bag

line

Throw bag

To prime the throw bag, fill it with rocks and tighten the drawstring.

NUTRITION

Eating well is the key to good health. This is especially true if you are getting active outdoors. Make sure you get a balanced intake of water, various food groups, vitamins, and minerals.

Water

The most vital substance in our bodies is water. It makes up more than half of a person's body weight, and fulfills such important roles that even a few days without it can be fatal.

BEAR SAYS

On days when you are active you will need more food and water than usual. Always stay hydrated, especially in hot weather.

Micronutrients

Micronutrients are essential vitamins and minerals that are needed in very small quantities for different body functions. Examples include salt, and the vitamins and minerals found in leafy vegetables, fruit, and vitamin supplements.

Carbohydrates

Carbohydrates are the body's main energy source. They are found in bread, pasta, rice, potatoes, fruit, and sweets.

Fats

Fats are essential for processing some vitamins, promoting healthy cell function, and are a rich source of energy.

Protein

Protein builds up, maintains, and replaces body tissues. It is essential for muscle growth and a healthy immune system.

Healthy eating

This is a graphic guide to a healthy meal. You should have more fruit and vegetables than any other food group. Cut down on big portion sizes, extra fats, and foods that are high in sugar and salt.

fats and sweets

milk, yogurt, and cheese

meat, poultry, fish, and nuts

vegetables

fruit

bread, cereal, rice, and pasta

FOOD FOR THE OUTDOORS

A healthy diet is essential when you are enjoying the outdoors. When planning a trip, choose food that is healthy, tasty, lightweight, and doesn't need to be refrigerated.

Hiking fuel

If you're on a big hike, your body will need a lot more food than normal. Graze on these easily digested, energy-rich foods to keep you going for hours.

trail mix: nuts, dried fruit, raisins, and seeds

cookies

chocolate

crackers

cereal bar

candy

Breakfast

cereal

oatmeal

powdered milk

shelf-stable milk

eggs

fruit

tea & coffee

bacon

bagels

pancakes

Lunch

bread
cheese
salami
crackers
powdered
fruit drink
sardines
banana
bread
vegetables
fruit
jam

Dinner

soup mix
rice
potatoes
pasta
beans
tea & coffee
couscous
herbs and
spices
cheese
tomato paste
salami
vegetables

Dessert

muffin
chocolate
hot
chocolate
fruit crumble
toasted
marshmallows

FIRE MAKING

Humans have been making and cooking on campfires for thousands of years. Making fire is still an important skill to have, so that you can stay warm and cook when camping.

Fire triangle

There are three elements that must be present for a fire to exist: oxygen, fuel, and heat. You need them in the right combination to get your fire started. Removing one or more of these elements will put out the fire.

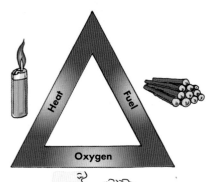

Tinder

Tinder is a fine, flammable material that easily catches a spark.

Bark
Look for dry inner bark from dead logs.

Moss
Dead, dry moss makes an excellent fire starter.

Grass
Break down stalks of dry grass into fine fibers.

Fungus
The inner flesh from bracket fungus is flammable.

Cotton balls and petroleum jelly
A highly flammable mix.

Leaves
Dry, dead leaves are often easy to find.

Parts of a fire

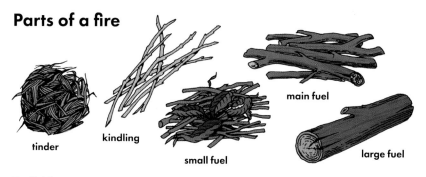

tinder

kindling

small fuel

main fuel

large fuel

Build it up

A good fire is built up gradually. Start with tinder, then once the tinder has begun to burn, add kindling—dry twigs and sticks no thicker than your little finger. As coals are created, slowly add larger pieces of fuel.

Starting structures

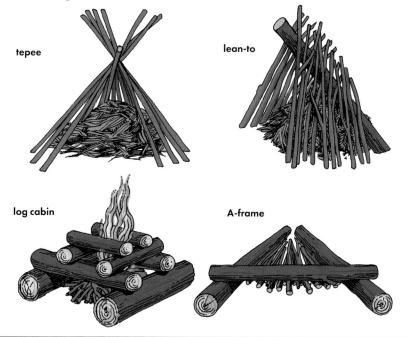

tepee

lean-to

log cabin

A-frame

FIRE STARTING

Starting fires has been a straightforward task ever since the invention of matches and lighters. However, there are other ways to create a spark if you don't have these tools available.

BEAR SAYS

Flint can be used to start fires even when wet, making it an incredibly useful piece of gear.

Heat sources

lighter

matches

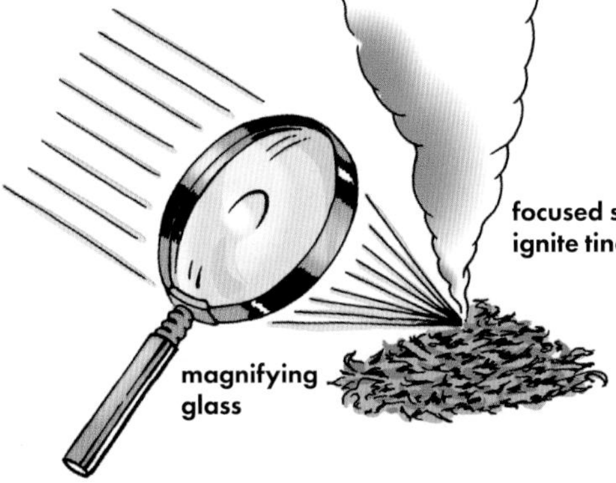

focused sunlight will ignite tinder
magnifying glass

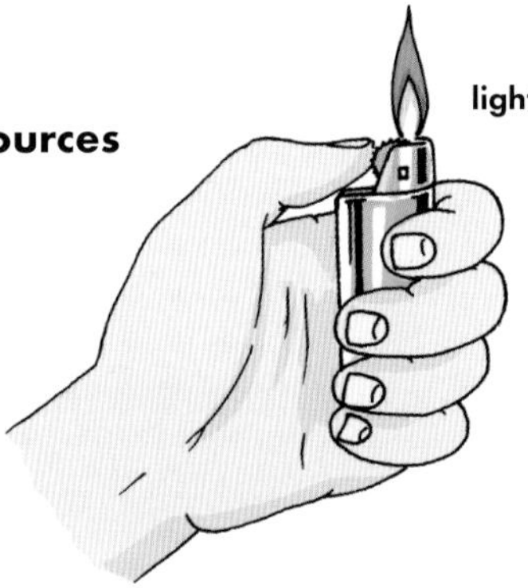

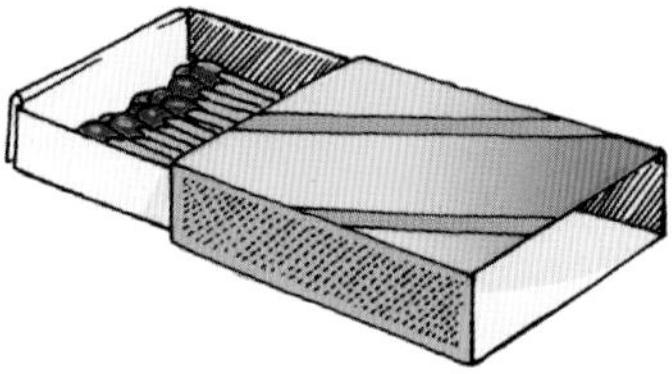

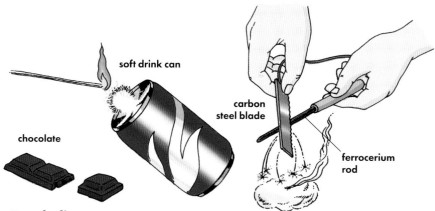

soft drink can

carbon steel blade

chocolate

ferrocerium rod

Parabolic can

Polish the base of a can with chocolate or toothpaste until it is mirror smooth and highly reflective (this may take several hours).

Flint and steel

The "flint" component of a flint and steel fire-starting kit is actually made of a metal alloy called ferrocerium. When struck with steel, it gives out sparks.

Battery method

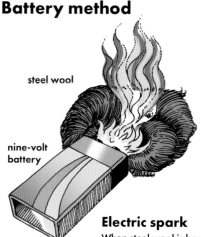

steel wool

nine-volt battery

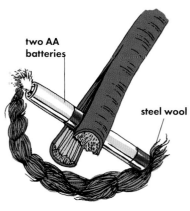

two AA batteries

steel wool

Electric spark

When steel wool is brushed against the contacts of a battery, it will glow brightly and begin to burn. A nine-volt battery is most convenient for this method, but any battery will work, including one from a mobile phone.

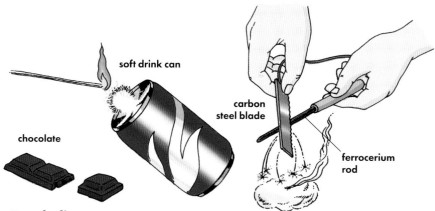

Magnesium fire block

These fire-starting kits consist of a steel striker and a block of magnesium with a ferrocerium rod fixed down one side. They are small and light, and are still effective in damp conditions.

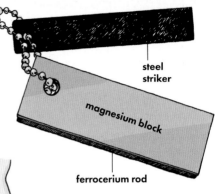

steel striker

magnesium block

ferrocerium rod

1 To begin, use a knife blade to scrape a small pile of shavings from the magnesium block. The shavings are light, so protect the pile from the breeze.

2 Collect the shavings and gather them in a little nest of dry tinder.

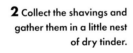

3 Run the ferrocerium rod along the steel striker or a knife blade. The resulting sparks will catch in the magnesium shavings and burn a very intense, white-hot flame for a few seconds—long enough to get your tinder burning.

Hand drill

A hand drill consists of a softwood
drill and fireboard. Run your hands
down the drill as you spin it to maintain
pressure and build friction.

Fire piston

This ancient device is from Southeast Asia
and the Pacific Islands. Quickly pushing the
piston into the cylinder causes a spark to be
ignited in the tinder.

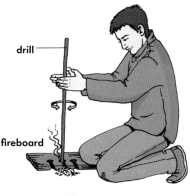

drill

fireboard

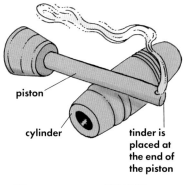

piston

cylinder

tinder is
placed at
the end of
the piston

tinder

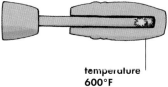

temperature
600°F

Fire plow

Cut a straight groove along a softwood base.
Plow the tip of a hardwood rod back and forth
along this groove. As friction builds up, small
wood fibers will become detached from the
groove. Eventually the detached
fibers will start smoldering and
form a "coal." Use this to
ignite your tinder.

smoldering
fibers

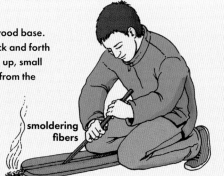

Bow drill

The bow drill is slightly more complicated than other friction fire-starting methods, but it is extremely effective.

spindle

bow

cord or leather thong

fireboard

tinder

notch cut in baseboard to hold tinder

Blowing tinder

The end result of many fire-starting methods is not a flame but a precious glowing ember. To really get the fire started, quickly gather the ember into a bundle of tinder and blow gently. This adds oxygen and raises the temperature enough for the material to burn.

Carrying fire

It can be easier to carry embers rather than to start a fire without matches or a lighter. To do this, punch a few holes in a can and attach a string or wire for a handle. Then place the embers between two layers of dry moss. Check the embers from time to time, and blow on them if they are starting to fade. If well cared for, the embers should last several days.

moss
embers
moss

COOKING WITH FIRE

As well as providing warmth and a place to gather, the main purpose of a campfire is to cook your food.

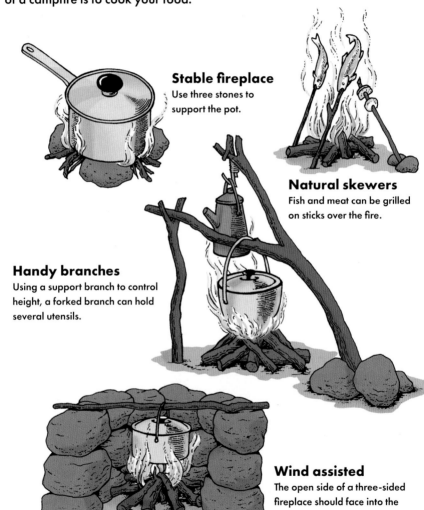

Stable fireplace
Use three stones to support the pot.

Natural skewers
Fish and meat can be grilled on sticks over the fire.

Handy branches
Using a support branch to control height, a forked branch can hold several utensils.

Wind assisted
The open side of a three-sided fireplace should face into the wind.

Basic construction

Put two logs parallel to the wind to form a simple fireplace.

An easy spit

Sharpened branches driven into the ground offer a sturdy spit.

Uneven surface

Use the slope of the ground and some large rocks to help support your utensils over the fire.

Longer term

If you are staying in one place for a while, dig a hole for a more permanent fireplace.

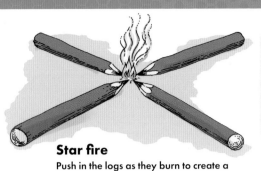

Star fire
Push in the logs as they burn to create a long-lasting cooking spot.

Crane
This arrangement will keep your cooking pot off the fire, and stop it from being smothered.

Adjustable crane
This crane allows you to move your pot up and down so that you can control the temperature it is exposed to.

Stone griddle
A slab of stone will take a long time to heat, but will also stay hot for a long time. Use a dry, solid rock.

Bamboo cooking pot

Green bamboo is very fire resistant and makes an excellent pot for boiling and simmering.

Bamboo steamer

Punch a few holes in each of the two walls that divide a length of bamboo into three sections. Put water in one end and food in the other—you have a steamer.

food goes here

steam

water

Breakfast in a bag

Line the bottom of a damp paper bag with bacon, then crack an egg on top. Place the bag on some hot coals and ashes to cook.

Foil oven

Wrap a whole meal in tinfoil and put it into the coals for a slow roast. By using this method exclusively, you can save on the weight of cooking pots and pans.

Hangi

The hangi is a traditional New Zealand Maori method of cooking large communal meals. To make a hangi, first dig a pit in the ground. Then build a pyre of wood beams over the pit to carry the hangi stones. Set the pyre ablaze to superheat the stones. Once they have dropped into the pit, add the food in wire baskets, cover in damp sacks and soil, and leave to cook for two to three hours.

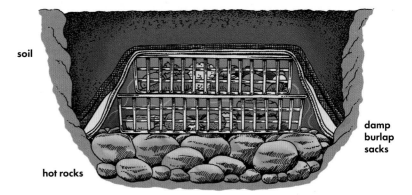

soil

damp burlap sacks

hot rocks

Mud baking

1 Gut a fish and lay it on a bed of nonpoisonous green leaves. There is no need to remove the scales.

2 Fold the leaves over the fish, ensuring that it is completely covered. Bind the package with twine.

3 Pack mud all around the package. Use clay if it is available, or use mud that has a claylike texture. Check for holes.

4 Bury the package in hot coals. A medium-sized fish should take about 20 minutes to cook.

CAMPING STOVES

Cooking meals on an open fire has its downsides. Things get sooty, and it can be hard to find fuel. Often, a camping stove is the best way to cook outdoors.

Fuel stoves

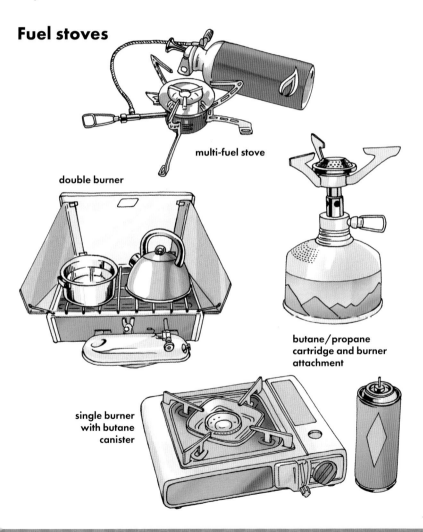

multi-fuel stove

double burner

butane/propane
cartridge and burner
attachment

single burner
with butane
canister

Alcohol burner set

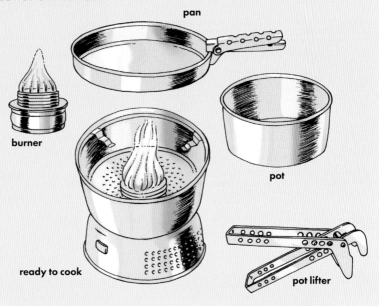

pan

burner

pot

ready to cook

pot lifter

Primus paraffin stove

Invented in 1892, the Primus pressurized paraffin burner was the original camping and expedition stove.

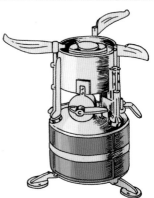

US Army gasoline-burning stove

These stoves were standard US Army issue from 1951 until 1987.

Cooking without gas

Parabolic solar cooker
Solar cookers are the ultimate in
environmentally friendly cooking.
Parabolic cookers can reach high
temperatures very quickly and are
good for bringing liquids to a boil.

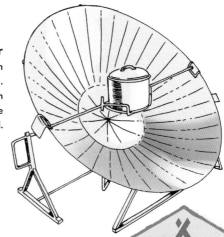

Twig stove
This low-impact
twig burner can be
easily made from a
steel can and wire
using basic tools.

✕ BEAR SAYS
If you are prepared, cooking
in the wild can be easy. Be
extra careful with camping
stoves, however, as they
can reach extreme
temperatures.

Solar box oven
This design makes use of
reflective panels and a sealed
light-absorbent chamber.
Temperatures inside can
reach 300°F.

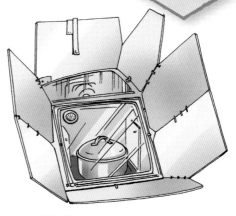

Discover all the books in the
Bear Grylls Outdoor Skills Handbook series:

Hiking Adventures

Dangers and Emergencies

Shelter Building

Dangerous Animals

Campfire Cooking

Going Camping

Kane Miller, A Division of EDC Publishing, 2024

Bonnier Books UK in partnership with Bear Grylls Ventures
Produced by Bonnier Books UK
Copyright © 2018 Bonnier Books UK

For information contact:

Kane Miller, A Division of EDC Publishing

5402 S 122nd E Ave

Tulsa, OK 74146

www.kanemiller.com | www.paperpie.com
Library of Congress Control Number: 2023944005

Printed in China
1 2 3 4 5 6 7 8 9 10

ISBN: 978-1-68464-920-4

Disclaimer
Bonnier Books UK, Bear Grylls, and Kane Miller take pride in doing their best to get the facts right in
putting together the information in this book, but occasionally something slips past us. Therefore, we
make no warranties about the accuracy or completeness of the information in the book and to the
maximum extent permitted, we disclaim all liability. Wherever possible, we will endeavor to correct
any errors of fact at reprint.

Kids—if you want to try any of the activities in this book, please ask your parents first! Parents—all outdoor
activities carry some degree of risk and we recommend that anyone participating in these activities be
aware of the risks involved and seek professional instruction and guidance. None of the health/medical
information in this book is intended as a substitute for professional medical advice; always seek the advice
of a qualified practitioner.